A Moon for Moe and Mo

A Moon for Moe and Mo

Jane Breskin Zalben

Illustrated by Mehrdokht Amini

Charlesbridge

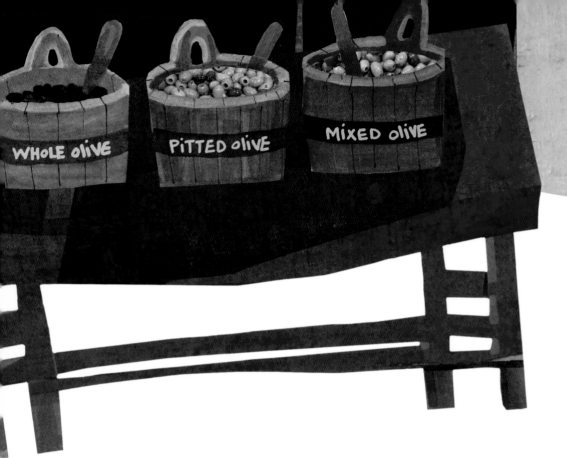

For Penny, who loves me almost as much as Sahadi's chocolate raisins, but whom I love more than the sun, moon, and stars. And to where it all began in Brooklyn many generations ago.—J. B. Z.

For Mum, Dad, and Mani—M. A.

Published by Charlesbridge, 85 Main Street,
Watertown, MA, 02472
(617) 926-0329 • www.charlesbridge.com

Printed in China
(hc) 10 9 8 7 6 5 4 3 2 1

Illustrations done in acrylic, markers, ink, photo collage, and then digitally assembled in Photoshop
Display type set in Wanderlust Boho
Text type set in Grenadine
Color separations by Colourscan Print Co. Ltd., Singapore
Printed by 1010 Printing International Limited in Huizhou, Guangdong, China
Production supervision by Brian G. Walker
Designed by Susan Mallory Sherman

Library of Congress Cataloging-in-Publication Data
Names: Zalben, Jane Breskin, author. | Amini, Mehrdokht, illustrator.
Title: A moon for Moe and Mo / Jane Breskin Zalben ; illustrated by Mehrdokht Amini.
Description: Watertown, MA : Charlesbridge, [2018] | Summary: Moses Feldman and Mohammed Hassan both live on Flatbush Avenue, but when they meet at the grocery store they quickly become best friends, sharing a picnic while their families prepare for the holidays of Rosh Hashanah and Ramadan.
Identifiers: LCCN 2016009219 (print) | LCCN 2016027157 (ebook) | ISBN 9781632895790 (ebook) | ISBN 9781632895806 (ebook pdf) | ISBN 9781580897273 (reinforced for library use)
Subjects: LCSH: Jewish families—New York (State)—Kings County—Juvenile fiction. | Muslim families—New York (State)—Kings County—Juvenile fiction. | Friendship—Juvenile fiction. | Cultural pluralism—New York (State)—Kings County—Juvenile fiction. | Flatbush Avenue (New York, N.Y.)—Juvenile fiction. | Brooklyn (New York, N.Y.)—Juvenile fiction. | CYAC: Jews—United States—Fiction. | Muslims—Fiction. | Friendship— Fiction. | Brooklyn (New York, N.Y.)—Fiction.
Classification: LCC PZ7.Z254 (ebook) | LCC PZ7.Z254 Mo 2018 (print) | DDC [E]—dc23
LC record available at https://lccn.loc.gov/2016009219

ICE

BOXES

00

MINT

Hot Cu   STAR ANISE   TURMERIC   RED PEPPER

Moses Feldman lived at one end of Flatbush Avenue,

and **Mohammed Hassan** lived at the other.

One fall day each boy went with his mother to a store right in the middle of the avenue. Bells tinkled when they went inside.

The air smelled of spices and fresh teas.
Baskets were filled with apricots, figs, dates,
nuts, and pomegranates bursting with seeds
that glistened like little red jewels.

Each boy ran down the market's aisles.
When Moses grabbed powdered candies,
Mrs. Feldman cried out, "Moe, don't touch!"
As sweet nougats tumbled off a shelf,
Mrs. Hassan warned, "Mo, be more careful!"

Moe and Mo turned around
and stared at each other.
Sugar dusted their noses,
cheeks, and fingers.

ISFAHAN PISTACHIO NOUGATS

PICKLES AND CHUTNEYS

100 % Natural ingredients

HOMEMADE PRESERVES

MIXED OLIVE

PITTED OLIVE

WHOLE OLIVE

82

BROOKLYN

JELLY BEANS

"Are you twins?" asked Mr. Sahadi, the store owner. "Or cousins?" Each boy shook his head no.

Moe peered at Mo's curly dark hair
and brown eyes.
Just like his.

Mo noticed Moe's olive skin
and shy smile.
Just like his.

Mr. Sahadi handed each boy
a piece of thick taffy.
"Thank you," they said together,
both grinning widely.

"Do you live around here?" asked Mo.
Moe pointed down the street one way.
"I live here, too," said Mo, pointing the other way.

Moe bounced his favorite ball—the pink rubber
one that had lots of bounce—toward Mo.
Mo bounced it back. Back and forth it went
until it rolled behind Mr. Sahadi's counter.

"I think *this* kind of ball is better in a food store," said Mr. Sahadi. He gave them each a large falafel ball—still warm—stuffed inside fluffy pita bread.

"I'm so full, I feel like I swallowed a big bowling ball,"
Moe said after he took his last bite.
"Me, too," said Mo, patting his stomach.

While Mrs. Feldman waited with her basket,
Mrs. Hassan waited with hers.

When it was time to go, the boys waved.
"See you soon!" they called out.
But they didn't.

Weeks passed.

Mrs. Feldman was getting ready for Rosh Hashanah,
the holiday celebrating the new year.
As she made a brisket and rugelach,
Moe got pastry dough everywhere.
"Enough, Moe," sighed Mrs. Feldman.

Mrs. Hassan was preparing for Ramadan,
the holiest month of the year.
As she roasted lamb and mixed date cookies,
Mo spilled chopped dates on the floor.
"Enough, Mo," sighed Mrs. Hassan.

Finally their mothers decided to take a break
and brought each boy to the park.
The boys were surprised to see each other.

"Race you to the playground!" yelled Moe.
"On your mark! Get set, go!" Mo yelled back.
They climbed, swung, and played hide-and-seek.

Meanwhile both mothers glanced
around the crowded playground.
Where were Moe and Mo?

Mrs. Feldman ran in circles. "Moe! Moe!"
Mrs. Hassan was also frantic. "Mo! Mo!"
Fearful moments felt like endless hours.

They decided to search together.
That's when they found Moe and Mo.
Happy and muddy, the boys looked up from digging.
Each mother held her son and cried tears of joy.

"You are the sun, moon, and stars,"
Mrs. Hassan said to Mo.
"And everything in between,"
Mrs. Feldman said to Moe.
And then the mothers hugged each other.

As they all walked home, Moe and Mo asked,
"Can we have a picnic in the park later?"
Both mothers nodded.

At sundown they feasted under a leafy tree.
Mo brought date cookies crumbled with almonds.
Moe brought rugelach rolled with raisins.
"Shalom," said Moe's family, wishing peace.
"Salaam," said Mo's family, wishing peace.

That night the first sliver of the moon shone down on Moe. He looked out his bedroom window and whispered to the starry sky, "A blessed Ramadan, Mo."

Mo also looked out his bedroom window and whispered into the moonlit night, "Happy New Year, Moe."

And the same moon watched over
both boys as they slept—

Moe at one end of Flatbush Avenue, and Mo at the other.

Rosh Hashanah

Rosh Hashanah is the Jewish New Year, and the words mean "head of the year" in Hebrew. It begins on the night of the New Moon in the seventh month of the Hebrew calendar. Families greet each other with "L'Shanah Tovah! To a good year!" The shofar—a trumpet made from a ram's horn—is blown in traditional communities every morning for the entire month before Rosh Hashanah. The sound calls people together to hear the Ten Commandments in the synagogue. Many attend services where the Torah, a holy scroll of laws and customs, is read to guide the congregation on how to lead a good life.

During the holiday, tzedakah (charity gifts) of food and money are given to help the needy. Round challah bread (for the cycle of life), apples dipped in honey (for a sweet year), and pomegranates (for a bountiful life) are part of the holiday meal. Rugelach is a dessert that is often served.

The ten days starting with Rosh Hashanah and ending with Yom Kippur are called the High Holy Days or the Days of Awe. Yom Kippur, the Day of Atonement, is the most solemn day of the Jewish year. People fast and pray until sundown. Afterward, a light dairy meal called a "break fast" is enjoyed with family and friends.

Rugelach

Moe's family loves these pastries with a cup of tea with lemon and honey. Moe always makes this recipe with adult assistance and supervision. Preparation time depends on the person, but plan on at least two hours. Each batch of rugelach takes time to fill, roll, and bake. This recipe makes 3 dozen.

FLOUR
100%
ALL-PURPOSE
FLOUR

FRESH
BREAD

Dough

2 sticks (1 cup) unsalted butter, softened to room temperature
1 8-ounce package of cream cheese, softened to room temperature
½ teaspoon vanilla extract
2 tablespoons orange zest (grated fresh orange rind or store bought, optional)
½ teaspoon salt (optional)
2 cups unbleached flour, sifted

Filling

²/₃ cup chopped walnuts, finely ground (optional)
¹/₃ cup granulated sugar
½ cup raisins or currants
1 teaspoon cinnamon

Other Ingredients

1 cup strawberry, red-raspberry, or marmalade jam
1 ½-ounce bag of mini chocolate chips (optional)

You can make the dough the night before, or you can freeze one or two of the dough balls to use at another time.

1. In a mixer, cream the butter and the cream cheese together, and add the vanilla extract and orange zest.
2. Add the salt to the flour.
3. Gradually add the flour to the creamed mixture, and blend all ingredients.
4. When a sticky dough is formed, knead it into a ball on a floured surface. Wrap the dough in waxed paper. Refrigerate until it hardens, approximately 2 hours.
5. Preheat the oven to 350°F.
6. Remove the dough from the refrigerator and divide it into 3 parts. With a rolling pin, roll one section of the dough at a time on a floured surface until it is about ¹/₈-inch thick. Place a large pie plate upside down on top of the dough. Cut around the outer edge with a knife. Discard the extra dough. (You can save it to patch any holes later on.) Repeat for the other two parts of dough.
7. In a small bowl, mix together the filling ingredients. Set aside.
8. Spread your jam of choice on the circular dough surfaces with a spatula.
9. Sprinkle ¹/₃ of the filling mixture across each of the three jam-covered doughs. Add some chocolate chips. With a pizza cutter or knife cut each circle into 12 triangles (like a pizza). Roll each piece into a crescent shape. Sprinkle with the extra filling mixture.
10. Place on greased or parchment-lined cookie sheets.
11. Bake for 20 minutes or until the rugelach is a light tan and the bottom of the pastry is still soft.

Ramadan

Ramadan begins when the first Crescent Moon appears on the ninth month of the Islamic calendar. Families greet each other in Arabic, "Eid Mubarak! Have a happy and blessed Eid." Muslims celebrate with a month of fasting (sawm) each day from dawn to sunset, and often break their fast (called iftar) by eating dates. One-thirtieth of the Qur'an (Koran) is recited each night in prayers, so by the end of the month the Muslim holy book is completely read.

During the holiday, food is donated to the poor in what's known as Zakat al-Fitr. The festival of Eid al-Fitr marks the end of Ramadan and lasts for three days of forgiveness, prayer, unity, and peace. Many go to a mosque where the Qur'an is read, telling the story of Mohammed the Prophet and his journey from Mecca to Medina. Families visit friends and relatives to break the fast. Different foods are eaten in different countries, since there are many Muslims throughout the world.

Date Cookies

Mo's family loves to munch on these treats with a glass of sweet mint tea. Mo always makes this recipe with adult assistance and supervision. Preparation time depends on the person, but plan on about two hours. Each batch of date cookies takes time to mix and bake. This recipe makes 3 dozen.

Ingredients

2 cups unbleached flour, sifted
1 teaspoon baking powder
½ teaspoon ground cardamom
½ teaspoon salt
¾ cup butter, melted
1 cup granulated sugar
3 large eggs, beaten
1 cup pitted dates, chopped
pinch of lemon zest (freshly grated lemon rind, optional)
1 cup slivered or chopped almonds (or grated pistachios or walnuts, optional)
36 whole blanched almonds to decorate each cookie

Preheat oven to 350°F.

1. Sift the flour and baking powder together.
2. Add the cardamom and salt. Set aside in a small bowl.
3. Beat together the butter, sugar, and eggs. Add the optional lemon zest.
4. In a large mixer or food processor, mix all the ingredients together until a soft dough is formed, adding a little water if it seems too dry.
5. Blend in the dates and almonds.
6. Scoop heaping teaspoons of the dough an inch apart on greased or parchment-lined baking sheets.
7. Put one whole almond on top of each cookie or sprinkle the chopped almonds, finely grated pistachios, or walnuts as a dusting on each cookie.
8. Bake 15 minutes or until cookies turn golden brown. Remove and allow to cool before serving.

Author's Note

A New Moon marks the beginning of each month in the lunar calendar, which both the Hebrew and Muslim calendars follow. A New Moon looks like a very thin crescent in the night sky. Rosh Hashanah is usually in September. Ramadan can take place at different times of the year. Rosh Hashanah and Ramadan occur at the same time roughly every thirty years, like the year in this story when Moe and Mo meet and celebrate together.

The inspiration for this book brewed over the years after I was invited to visit schools in Ethiopia, Egypt, Israel, Morocco, Spain, and Turkey. I experienced many ancient mosques and synagogues and appreciated the beauty of both. I also learned that the Hebrew and Arabic words for compassion, *rahamim* (Hebrew) and *rahma* (Arabic), share the same root. Compassion is the foundation of any good friendship.

The final spark that made me write Moe and Mo's story was food shopping for Jewish holidays in Islamic and Hasidic neighborhoods in Brooklyn.

Illustrator's Note

I spent the best moments of my childhood in a small garden in a small city surrounded by glorious mountains in a faraway land.

My cousin often came to play with me, and together we imagined that behind the mountains there was a magical land where fairies and jinns lived. We used to dig under my father's precious rose bushes in search of buried treasures. We argued a lot over how to kill the giant jealous snake who was guarding the treasure and occasionally fought over how to divide the gold once we found it! We climbed the trees and planned to make a house up on the branches just the way Huckleberry Finn did in his adventures.

Years passed by and I never set foot in the magical land behind the mountains, nor did I find the buried treasures or manage to build the tree house like Huck did.

I grew up and learned that adults have more serious matters to deal with. That is, until the day I decided to become a children's book illustrator. Once again I found myself in the parallel world of dreams and magic, and now I had an excuse to be there.

When I read the story of Moe and Mo, I was overjoyed by the possibility of working on a book about empathy, the beauty of similarities, and the ease with which children form deep friendships.

Stereotyping usually exists in the world of adults, while children see the world in a more accepting and unbiased way.